Daniel and the Nutcracker

Adapted by Angela C. Santomero

Additional writing by Alexandra Cassel

Based on the screenplay "Neighborhood Nutcracker"
written by Jill Cozza-Turner

Poses and layouts by Jason Fruchter

Simon Spotlight

New York   London   Toronto   Sydney   New Delhi

It's a snowy day in the Neighborhood of Make-Believe, and Daniel Tiger is so excited for winter! Today he is going to the Enchanted Garden to see his friends perform in a winter ballet called the *Nutcracker*, where a toy nutcracker comes to life and dances.

Daniel dances around the room like the Nutcracker. *"March, march, march!"* sings Daniel. Pretending to be the Nutcracker is so much fun! Daniel wonders which one of his friends is going to be the Nutcracker in the show!

Daniel and Dad slosh through the snow to the Enchanted Garden. As they march like Nutcrackers, they sing. *"We're going to the Enchanted Garden to see the* Nutcracker *show. Won't you march along with me? March along!"*

"Who is going to be the Nutcracker in the show?" Daniel asks Dad. But Dad's not sure. Daniel will have to wait to find out.

Daniel meets his friend O the Owl at the Enchanted Garden. Together, they press the three red roses and the gate opens. Inside they see a beautiful stage decorated with twinkly white lights. Daniel is so excited!

"Come on, O," says Daniel. "Let's go sit down to see the show!"

O the Owl does not want to go inside to see the show. O is scared.

Daniel can see that his friend is nervous. He gives O a hug. He asks, "Why are you scared, O?"

With big wide eyes, O looks at his friend. He says, "Hoo, hoo. It is noisy and dark in there, and there are lots and lots of people. I don't think I want to go in and see the show anymore."

Uncle X kneels down next to O and says, "When something seems hard to do, try it a little bit at a time. Can you go inside a little bit at a time, O?" asks Uncle X.

O the Owl nods. He will try going in to the show, a little bit at a time. "Will you walk with me, Daniel?" he asks.

"Of course," says Daniel, taking O's wing. "Let's walk inside, together, a little bit at a time."

Holding hands, Daniel and O the Owl find their seats together. Trying it a little bit at a time helps O. He doesn't feel as scared. Now he's ready to see the show! Daniel feels proud of O. O feels proud too.

"Hey, look!" says Daniel Tiger, pointing. "It's Katerina Kittycat on the stage! She looks just like a ballet dancer in her tutu!" Daniel looks around for the Nutcracker. He wonders again who the Nutcracker is going to be. He asks, "Do you know, O?" But O shakes his head. He doesn't know.

Daniel really, really wants to know who is going to be the Nutcracker!

Katerina Kittycat wants to tell Daniel who the Nutcracker is. But he needs to go backstage to find out.

When he gets backstage, Daniel sees Prince Wednesday dressed as the Nutcracker. "Prince Wednesday! You are the Nutcracker?" asks Daniel.

"ACHOO!" Prince Wednesday sneezes. "I was excited to be the Nutcracker. But now I'm sick. I can't dance in the show as the Nutcracker. ACHOO!"

"Oh no," says Daniel. "Who will be the Nutcracker?"

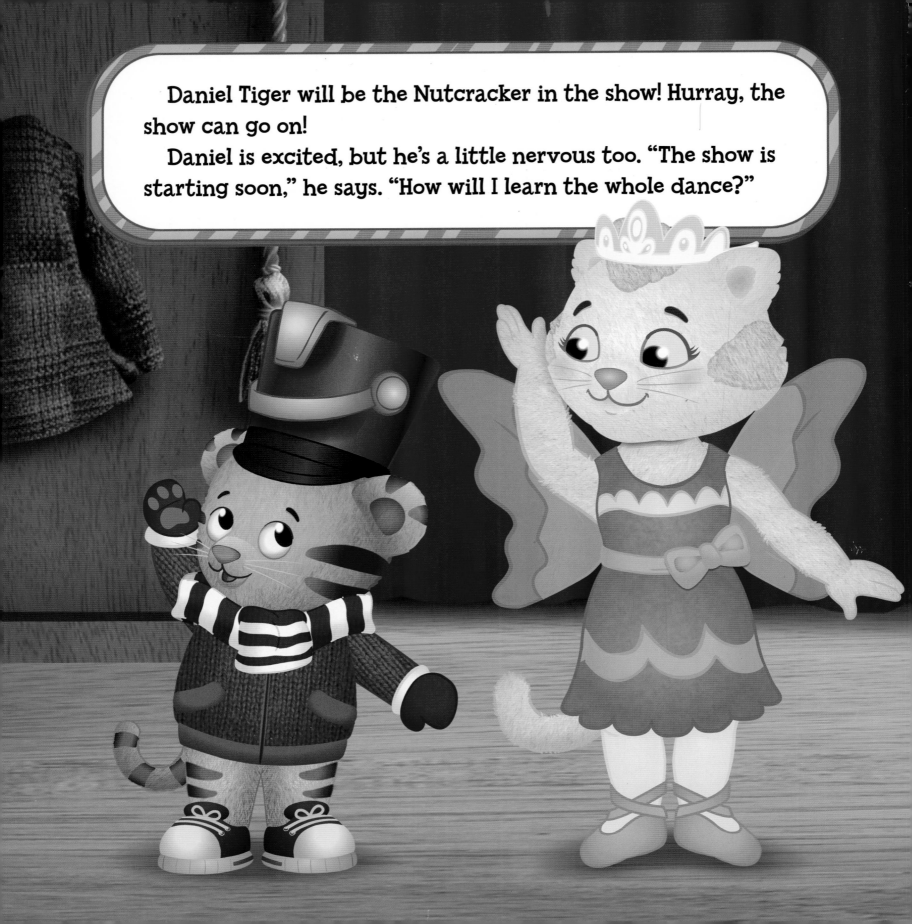

Daniel Tiger will be the Nutcracker in the show! Hurray, the show can go on!

Daniel is excited, but he's a little nervous too. "The show is starting soon," he says. "How will I learn the whole dance?"

Daniel sings to himself, "When something seems hard to do, try it a little bit at a time."

Katerina teaches Daniel the Nutcracker dance, a little bit at a time, and Daniel tries his very best. "One arm up. Then the other. Turn around, leap, and march, march, march!"

Daniel tries the dance a little bit at a time. "Will you do it with me?" Daniel asks. "One arm up. Then the other. Turn around, leap, and march, march, march!"

Soon Daniel feels ready. Let's start the show!

Once upon a time, there was a little girl named Clara.
O the Owl points to Katerina. "I see Clara, hoo hoo!"

Clara received a special toy soldier named the Nutcracker. One night, the toy nutcracker came alive and danced all by himself! The Nutcracker took a deep breath and tried with all his might. He leapt to the left, and he leapt to the right. Twirling and twirling, he gave Clara a spin.

"Look, hoo hoo!" says O. "That's Daniel Tiger!"

Clara and the Nutcracker went to the magical Land of Sweets where they met the Sugar Plum Fairy.

They all danced and danced and danced, and lived happily ever after.

"I didn't think I could do it, but then I did it, a little bit at a time," says Daniel Tiger. "I'm glad you were here to dance the *Nutcracker* ballet with me. Ugga Mugga!"